# THE LIGHT OF INVISIBLE BODIES

ALSO BY JEANNE LOHMANN

*Where the Field Goes,* 1976
*Steadying the Landscape,* 1982
*Gathering a Life,* 1989
*Between Silence and Answer,* 1994
*Granite Under Water,* 1996
*Flying Horses,* 2001
*Greatest Hits,* 1956–2000

# The Light of Invisible Bodies

POEMS

Jeanne Lohmann

*Jeanne Lohmann*

2003 · FITHIAN PRESS · MCKINLEYVILLE, CALIFORNIA

Some of these poems were published in the following journals: *Atlanta Review, The Bitter Oleander, Buffalo Spree, Convolvulus, Earthlight, Friends Journal, Generations, The Mennonite, Northwest Literary Forum, Poetry Northwest, Raven Chronicles, Runes, Saluti di Spoleto, Santa Barbara Review, Santa Clara Review, Sea Change, Snow Monkey, Transfer, Yankee, Zone 3.*

"Missing" is reprinted by permission of *Yankee Magazine*, March 1985. "Word of Honor" appears in the anthology *Proposing on the Brooklyn Bridge*. My thanks to the editors and publishers for permission to include this work.

Selected poems are from out-of-print collections, and from two chapbooks, *Gathering Stones* and *Ends of the Earth* (Newmarket Press).

Copyright © 2003 by Jeanne Lohmann
All rights reserved
Printed in the United States of America

Published by Fithian Press
A division of Daniel and Daniel, Publishers, Inc.
Post Office Box 2790
McKinleyville, CA 95519
www.danielpublishing.com

LIBRARY OF CONGRESS CATALOGING-IN-PUBLICATION DATA
Lohmann, Jeanne.
  The light of invisible bodies : poems / by Jeanne Lohmann.
    p. cm.
  ISBN 1-56474-426-4 (pbk. : alk. paper)
  1. Death—Poetry. 2. Grief—Poetry. 3. Nature—Poetry. I. Title.
  PS3562.O463L54 2003
  811'.54—dc21
          2003004005

*...there is no explaining
the dark, it is only the light
that we keep feeling a need to account for*

*—W.S. Merwin
from "The Marfa Lights"*

# Contents

## One

Properties of Light . . . . . . . . . . . . . . . . . . . . . . . . . . 11
Life Work . . . . . . . . . . . . . . . . . . . . . . . . . . . . . . . . . 12
Artist in a New Season . . . . . . . . . . . . . . . . . . . . . . . 13
Green Pond in April . . . . . . . . . . . . . . . . . . . . . . . . . 14
After a Southern Visit . . . . . . . . . . . . . . . . . . . . . . . 15
Rituals at the Farm . . . . . . . . . . . . . . . . . . . . . . . . . 16
Across the Road . . . . . . . . . . . . . . . . . . . . . . . . . . . 18
Autumn Fruit . . . . . . . . . . . . . . . . . . . . . . . . . . . . . 19
Field Notes: The Blue Ridge Mountains . . . . . . . . . 20
On the Porch . . . . . . . . . . . . . . . . . . . . . . . . . . . . . 22
Night, and the House Has a Voice . . . . . . . . . . . . . . 23
Rivertalk . . . . . . . . . . . . . . . . . . . . . . . . . . . . . . . . . 24

## Two

The Logicians . . . . . . . . . . . . . . . . . . . . . . . . . . . . . 27
Manzanar . . . . . . . . . . . . . . . . . . . . . . . . . . . . . . . . 28
Lobelia . . . . . . . . . . . . . . . . . . . . . . . . . . . . . . . . . . 30
Part of Me . . . . . . . . . . . . . . . . . . . . . . . . . . . . . . . 32
Black Water Going Under . . . . . . . . . . . . . . . . . . . 33
Tracking the Dead . . . . . . . . . . . . . . . . . . . . . . . . . 34
Early Morning, the Cold House . . . . . . . . . . . . . . . 35
How It Goes On . . . . . . . . . . . . . . . . . . . . . . . . . . 36
What the Day Gives . . . . . . . . . . . . . . . . . . . . . . . . 37
Happiness . . . . . . . . . . . . . . . . . . . . . . . . . . . . . . . 38
Missing . . . . . . . . . . . . . . . . . . . . . . . . . . . . . . . . . 39
Toward Dance . . . . . . . . . . . . . . . . . . . . . . . . . . . . 40
Sunset, the Sierra . . . . . . . . . . . . . . . . . . . . . . . . . . 41
Ways to Be Unimportant . . . . . . . . . . . . . . . . . . . . 42
Meditation Cabin: The Poet Studies the Walls . . . . . 43
Northwest Winter . . . . . . . . . . . . . . . . . . . . . . . . . 44
Washing the Roots of the Mind . . . . . . . . . . . . . . . 45

## Three

| | |
|---|---|
| In the Medici Chapel | 49 |
| Where We Went When We Knew… | 50 |
| Not Lost | 52 |
| Italian Summer, Thinking of Blueberries | 53 |
| How Could You Not | 54 |
| Mysteries in Spoleto | 55 |
| Foreign Country, Home Country | 56 |

## Four

| | |
|---|---|
| Of Time and Light | 59 |
| September Day I Tell to No One | 60 |
| Awake | 62 |
| Word of Honor | 63 |
| Getting Ready to Move | 64 |
| Salt Water | 66 |
| Return | 67 |
| One Way or Another | 68 |
| Memory Train | 69 |
| After Eulogies | 70 |
| Full Stop in the Desert | 71 |
| Walking My Life | 72 |
| Spring Melt | 74 |

## Five

| | |
|---|---|
| Summons | 77 |
| Words That Wait to Be Said | 78 |
| Pittosporum | 80 |
| Falls River | 82 |
| Plum | 83 |
| Past Lives | 84 |
| For the Body | 85 |
| These Hours Like Making Love | 86 |
| Gratitude | 87 |
| After Traveling in Kyoto | 88 |
| Twilight, a Room on Russian Hill | 89 |
| Questions Before Dark | 90 |
| Praise What Comes | 91 |

*One*

*Properties of Light*

A field of light, and my need to say
that it exists. Each morning I walk here
almost blinded by water the sun shines on,
look down from Strawberry Hill
across the roofs of the dazzling city
emerging out of fog, a haze of light
over and around the houses, giving
everything a quality for which *luminous*
is the only word. My need to see such light
holding and sliding off the eucalyptus trunks,
their ragged bark. To be exposed to the wet grasses
shaking and splintering that light, to recognize
nasturtium leaves for the bright green mirrors
they are, the red, orange and yellow fires
inextinguishable, spreading up the hill.

Limestone and granite give back radiance, and we
walkers in this field lift our feet and set out,
moving through our once and only mornings,
afternoons. Light searches the surfaces of all things,
and what if there were no mirrors in the world, what if
the brass lock on the door did not say no, the window
did not let the light come through? What if light
did not find itself renewable? As my necessity
for these words, mirrors I carry into the sun
of this blazing day, this dance, this carnival
where I am given access to another world,
to the spirits who walk with me
pointing out the properties of light.

*Life Work*

The softening underfoot, a perceptible shift
in the ground, birds louder in the bare trees,
the light fluid as water. Winter is tired
and winding down, can't keep the temperature

falling toward zero. I will have to risk it,
surf the crest of spring, take the dangerous wave
into summer, as a woman in labor learns to go
with tides that open her body, as she breathes

in a different rhythm. Breathing ahead of pain
that rises when forsythia and heather tell me
how alive people I loved were when they died,
it's then I remember pain has a life of its own

as Pollock said a painting does on its way
into the world. Life work I care for, and let go.
Pushed into warmth and light, the hidden crocus
opens through dirt and duff, last year's leaves.

*Artist in a New Season*

Black stoneware plate. Orange segments
many small boats, citrus zinging my nose,

but what can I do with brush and paper,
with words, when new life pulls me

into fronds and leaves and the roots
are after my toes? Dust-red and gray

earthworms crawl into and over the ground.
Like confetti, seeds fly out of my hand.

This gauzy light tastes like wild strawberry,
a blossoming peach is enough.

And your eyes that listen as blue knows how,
your mouth that takes my tongue.

### Green Pond in April

If I go to a green pond in April,
will last year's muck and brown water
recede into layers at the bottom?

A dead fledgling in my hand,
will I see it as fluff and feathers,
feel *bird* in the small bones?

I'd like to learn not to care what happens
next, how to abandon the deathwatch
and enter the tomb that is and will be

always empty. Where silence begins,
to learn to let go, even where life
hurts most. Answer spring with *yes*.

*After a Southern Visit*

My aunt is epiphyte. She needs a tree
and could be orchid, fern or hanging moss.
Bromeliad, she pulls her food from air.
She lives attached, and holding on above the ground.

Rare white orchid with a golden mouth, she
blooms from a tough old base. Leaves strong as leather
thicken near the stem. They say this flower's lip
is marked to guide one special insect in.

They say resistant forms live highest in the trees.
one long exotic flowering and they die
leaving the young wild shoots. My aunt's green
aerial roots take care of what she needs.

She's fed by things that swim in atmosphere
and never moves away from home. What floats
about her is enough. She keeps reserve supplies.
When life dries up she waits a coming of the rains.

*Rituals at the Farm*

Climbing between ruts in the road to the upper field
I stop at the remembered place, make a pile of stones.
April wind shivers the stubble where hay-mower,
rake and harrow stand ready for this year's planting.
Breaking the brown stalks of milkweed pods
that split one side to parachute seed into air, I
pull a handful of oat grass, tie it all together,
put the spray next to the pile, weight it with pebbles.

At my feet the Husky, Jupa (named by a child trying
to say "You pup!"), lies down in the leaves. When I try
to say your name I can't for tears make the sound
come right. Nothing is left of the cairn I made
three years after your death, when clover, dandelion
and small daisies bloomed in the high field.
The trees rest in a green glow, the pale light of spring.

Below, on land beside the pond that red-winged
blackbirds fly over, a Cree medicine man is building
a sweat lodge for strangers who will bend and enter
hoping to be changed, healed by cedar smoke and herbs,
drumbeats in the dark, the ritual chanting.

Swamp willow cut for the framing
is bound with yellow twine, fire-stones
set in a circle. Deerskin pouches hang from poles,
eagle feathers. Watching the shaman work,
his surveyor's tape laid out on the ground, we
asked where we could walk. He looked in and through us,
took the cigarette from his mouth, pushed a pole
deeper into dirt, said, "It's all sacred."

Ahead of me on the downhill road, Jupa stops
distracted by deer scat, lifts her head to concentrate
on distance, the wooded valley. She is good company
on this walk through open fields, along the fenceline
of young pine and spruce, where I leave you
with wind through a bundle of oat grass,
the tough warty pods of milkweed,
empty of seeds.

*Across the Road*

a donkey wobbles ears, shakes tail,
kicks at the air in his green field

all morning that perfect and foolish
gray body moves without lies
the way bodies do
at home in pedestrian events

flame on a candlewick, my mind
asks how it would be
to be ready for death by not
thinking about it, a child

at the fenced-in field
with apples in her hands

*Autumn Fruit*

I'm learning now to wait and not to rush
the apple harvest, wait for dark brown seeds
to fill the membranes at the core, the ripening
blush that signals sweetness in the flesh
inside the crisp and tender skin. Windfalls
serve for sauce. I've pulled the smaller
fruit to help the branches bear the weight
of bigger apples coming on.

But I am new to harvest from these trees
and late to learn how often I have picked
my fruit too green and hoped in vain
the juice would rise and swell
against the stem, the cellar darkness
force the sour unready meat.

### *Field Notes: The Blue Ridge Mountains*

crossing the moon, the geese
too many to count
in the circular field the scope
brings in, this October light
so like spring the peepers
start courting

the goose in the lead
splits the wind
the formation follows

in the heron's shadow
fish turn into food

when you raise a shingle of shagbark hickory
a brilliant snake slides away

if you shift your eyes
light comes in
at intersections with dark

if you stay long enough
you can read under the full moon,
walk uneven ground
with high deliberate steps
over exposed roots and stones

tomorrow the maples
will burn scarlet when the sun
takes them, the night bones
of cinnamon fern turn warm,
deadwood decay into a feast

and I will begin
learning to say
what I see

## On the Porch

The wolf of evening comes to my door,
lifts a paw, whimpers to be let in.
Nobody is clever enough to fend him off.
I have stopped trying, as I have given up
helping the world go on. Evening is only
itself, an interval before dark when
I pause to listen and say to any animal
that finds my house, "It's time to come in."

*Night, and the House Has a Voice*

Before falling asleep, and pretending
to hold back the dark, I listen
to what the house is saying.

Already I am beginning to forget
its daytime voice when the house
wants me to do many things, says

you're responsible for this mess and
you have to put it right or you
won't sleep sweet and easy.

But now, with night over everything,
I am content and happy, listening
to what the house is saying; go to sleep,

day will come. You don't have to stay awake
and wait. Work will wait, work is patient
that way. Go to sleep. Don't even try

to catch your breath. It's already gone
ahead of you into the dark that covers
and hides and forgives: the unswept floor,
the neglected phone call, dishes in the sink.

*Rivertalk*

is whatever comes along,
practice always here while we

keep on shore, all the time
saying we want to get wet.

But the river has ways
of sound and light, ripples

and waves that tell us:
don't be so serious, tumble in

where nothing is finished or broken
and nothing asks to be fixed.

*Two*

*The Logicians*

if light ripples the soft edges of air
so they open like silk, as some insist

they do, the premises we keep do not
allow such rifts in ordinary cloud.

The possibility of mind unloosed,
relieved of thought, moving to rhythms

not of our making, does not concur
with synthesis we know. Offhand

we cannot bring to mind a time we saw
the closed world leap apart, wheels

turning in heaven, a descent of angels
on ladders. We don't remember when

we dream, and when we sleep, we shift
our weight, uneasy on the stone.

*Manzanar*

*1. The Photograph:*
*From Manzanar Looking to Mt. Williamson*

A hard landscape for the heart, Manzanar
where Ansel Adams stood in 1944 to make
his picture, and where American Japanese
citizens lived under the weight of hysteria.
His photograph frames the geometry of rocks.
The light veers off the density of stone,
then diffuses, spreads. Holding the photograph
another way, the boulders appear to move.

What draws me here is energy confined,
space that defines each granite slab
so fixed it can belong no other place.
Even in parallax there's center to the mass,
a balance point for stones that rest
in free-fall of the light reflected off inertia,
rocks that take such light years to wear down.


*2. Grandfather Kataoka: His Story*

Mariko is making a garden for us at Manzanar.
She insists it won't be like Ryoan-ji
though there are stones enough, more sand
and gravel than she needs. In her college
Mariko studied the white dwarf she tells us
is a small dense star that has exhausted
its nuclear fuel and shines from residual heat.

That's how Mariko describes us, the half-life
we have here, the waves of light passing
the edges of our opaque bodies. She says
a garden would cool us at the center,
eclipse the dark matter she thinks our lives
are made of. I think she wants some beauty
against the zero weight of leaving our lives
behind on Bainbridge dock. Many lives, too heavy
for our small suitcases. Mariko's garden gives her
the hope I do not have. She tries to teach me
language I do not understand. The garden I see
is the Silver Pavilion, Jisho-ji, the sand mound
in its center, the furrows reflecting moonlight.
I think of Kan-non, Goddess of Mercy, and of Jizo,
Guardian God of Children. I think of gardeners
who bend with bamboo rakes when they come
to shape the smooth white sand into waves
around stones of the thousand-year crane,
the ten-thousand-year turtle. This language Mariko
does not know. For me the gates of many temples
are open, the purple wisteria blossoms
mirrored in ponds of floating lilies, yellow iris,
and the harp sound of falling water. Temple gardeners
have their work and their devotions, as Mariko does.
Mine were stolen from me. The blowing sand
and Manzanar rocks make no order in my mind.
In Owens Valley the heat is heavy. The light burns.

*Lobelia*

Sometimes all you need is an opening: lobelia, for instance,
*Crystal Palace*, deepest blue with red foliage
at the base of an old tree. I'd forgotten how flowers
can take me somewhere else, even a name
referential, this herbaceous plant named for
a 15th century Flemish botanist. Flowers
that return me to my first sighting—
in a planter box on a foggy San Francisco avenue,
the same dark blue, in front of the house of friends.

Refugees from Europe in the thirties, Irèné, opera singer,
Hungarian and Jewish, Ernst, Austrian, a physician, they
came with seven dollars, his mother's violin,
one small suitcase. Learned the new language,
passed medical exams, set up practice in New England.
Thirty years after, when they moved to California, neighbors
and friends, patients cordoned off the street to say goodbye.

Years later, here in my Washington town, lobelia
surprises me, the low-growing blue flowers
still offering their story, this fragment:
thirty-seven members of Irèné's family
killed by the Nazis, an infant thrown from a window.

And her answer when someone dared ask
    *how could you*
        *did you ever*
            *learn to forgive*

in the stunned hush of the room, as from some dark place
none of us could go, she said:
    *it takes time and patience, much love around one*
        *we hardly ever go back to those times*
            *what lives in us we can hardly bear to remember*

Careful with the roots, I lift clumps of lobelia,
*Crystal Palace*, from sixpacks of plastic,
make openings in the earth
where I plant the flowers,
with water enough,
the right sort of shade.

*Part of Me*
      *September 11, 2001*

Part of me believes in this white candle I take to the altar,
the Methodist church open for prayer after apocalypse in the east,
the president's early call for retribution, and why do I
remember William Stafford's *Aunt Mabel,* her senator
talking war, and Aunt Mabel saying, "We didn't elect him that much."

Part of me believes in lighting candles in a small-town church
like the one I grew up in, as part of me
rejoices in clear September sun when
like the psalmist, I lift my eyes to the Oregon hills.

Part of me hurries to say good morning to anyone
on these unfamiliar streets, strangers I want to run to
and fold in my arms as brother, sister, believing as I do
in blessing our days on this good earth.

I believe God has many houses and we are temples walking,
and the ocean of light and darkness is one ocean.
Today the tide rages in flood, dark waves
drowning the sunlit water that is, perhaps,
still reachable, but out so far,
the great incoming breakers heavy with salt.

*Black Water Going Under*

there are lights you can't reach alone,
lost as you are, flailing arms in the swamp,
cypress keening overhead, Spanish moss
trailing witches' hair in the water,
going under you reach for any hand
from any boat, somebody to pull you in,
tell you it's all right to be alive and
where you are, better to struggle
out of black water up the slippery
green side of the boat and fall in,
better to unhinge the rusty lock and lean
into the splintered oar, pull your weight
toward the light

*Tracking the Dead*

Everything comes from and goes
somewhere, even what seems

utterly to vanish into
no-place. If you can't

follow the footprints
in the snow, if you come

to where they end
and have to turn around,

set your feet in the freezing
hollows, go as far as you can.

Sing to the snow
still coming down.

*Early Morning, the Cold House*

Though the taste of nightmares
is in your mouth, you are not alone
in this corner of the room where

it's too soon for the sun to come.
Whenever you wish you can call your
ghosts, say the names though you know

they can't come through the window
or the shutters where light slides in.
It's all right to know or not to know.

Neither they nor you are lost.
Pull the blanket to your shoulders
and drink the tea that coats

your ragged throat. Be comforted
by the pencil in your hand, and poems,
a smile that surprises you from

the past and says good morning,
harbinger of other arrivals, grace
that comes whether you ask or no.

## How It Goes On

opening: the door, the box, the womb, the mouth,
hyacinth bulbs pushing out of earth, primrose

and peony uncurling, leaf buds loosening,
brown water rising in rivers, the bay

so high you see the tide take the beach
on the curve ahead of you, and the child

pulls milk from the full breast, the new mother
wakes from four hours of sleep, her arms

repeating the lesson: this is how it goes on
in the body, the house with doors and windows,

the sea opening and closing, the womb,
the mouth and eyes, the heart.

*What the Day Gives*

Suddenly, sun. Over my shoulder
in the middle of gray November
what I hoped to do comes back,
asking.

Across the street the fiery trees
hold onto their leaves,
red and gold in the final months
of this unfinished year, they
offer blazing riddles.

In the frozen fields of my life
there are no shortcuts to spring,
but stories of great birds in migration
carrying small ones on their backs,
predators flying next to warblers
they would, in a different season, eat.

Stunned by the astonishing mix in this uneasy world
that plunges in a single day from despair
to hope and back again, I commend my life
to Ruskin's difficult duty of delight,
and to that most beautiful form of courage,
to be happy.

*Happiness*

Sitting on a bench in winter morning sun
and detached among my blessings,
watching people go by, waiting for
my lunch date, I was surprised by
three strangers with a camera who
stopped to ask me about happiness:
are you happy? what makes you happy?
on a scale of one to ten, where are you? what
do you need in the next few months to claim
a higher rating? I hadn't thought
on these weighty matters, hadn't set
my life in such order. I tried to be honest,
say how I felt, my off-the-cuff answers
provocative enough to extend the conversation,
which is how I found out who was sponsoring
this sample for local access TV. One man asked
what did I think about Jesus. Well, that turned us
to text and translation, how we interpret
scripture, flesh out our faith, what's living
in and around us, our presumptuous knowing
(I said) of God. Heady stuff for a park bench
in January. I wish I'd found grace on my tongue,
remembered the courage it takes to be happy,
how yesterday afternoon a dozen audacious
red-headed finches in my leafless apple tree
were quite enough to tip the scale toward ten.

*Missing*

Your house keys really are somewhere, your papers
exactly as you left them. You only think
the streets moved when you can't find the car.
When you try so hard to look you can't see.

Listen. There may be music for lost things
to come home by. Pick it up, why don't you,
the thin silver whistle fallen between cracks.
Over there. At the edge of the world.

## *Toward Dance*

so in love we are
with the robust joy of our lives
even our cries and our curses
a confusion of praise,

but try not to think of words,
attend if you will, if you can,
to silence
where the voice begins

try not to think of the trumpet
but of gold in the throat,

the bones of our feet
will be moving toward dance,
around us such elegant music
we never in this world could have chosen

## Sunset, the Sierra

A bruised expanse of sky, evergreens
at the horizon, black twigs, branches,
and I want to be part of the color, this drama,
but I'm not invited. It's not my day's end,
nothing more than sunset-watching,
my Oh and Ah caught on the quick intake
and release of breath. It's time to say this
clearly: how often I want to hold on
to purple and rose, the fine-etched patterns
of trees against the sky, how hard to accept
glory that fades, like this band of lemon light
that glows above the rising dark, the darkest purple
darkening black, the black mesh of branches
disappearing into dark, one tree indistinguishable
from another until the moon comes up, and the stars.

*Ways to Be Unimportant*

Helped this morning by the large soggy leaves
of the Empress tree, picking them off the ground

one by one out of the pachysandra, taking them
with weeds to the yard-waste bin, afterward

aching, tired in ways that have nothing
to do with thoughts, of which I have too many,

not many important. Last night's bath
soaked some of them clean away.

Be unimportant, water always tells me,
and the flat, disintegrating leaves.

*Meditation Cabin: The Poet Studies the Walls*

I want to be ordinary, my words
ordinary, no sermons in stone, no message
in a fortune cookie, no need to translate,

transform, interpret. Unburdened by
metaphor and simile, to work in timelines
of redwood and cedar like these

vanishing beetles and burrowers
leaving remnants of their hidden lives
in trails and hollows, pits in the planks

defining the walls, narrowing prints
left by the hungry, their tunnels and waves
an intricate design of ovals and arrows.

Nothing profound or intentional,
work come late into light,
cross-grained, rough-cut.

*Northwest Winter*

light-dazed moments
send me to my knees,
halo the darkest cedars,
shatter surface water
to silver

last light in puddles
reflecting the sky,
sunlight off the dullest metal

I don't want to know
too much, only enough
to be curious
about the simplest things,
on this wet overcast day
to go outside where such light
as there is
finds me, and falls
slantwise
through the rain

*Washing the Roots of the Mind*

They come up dangling, with the dirt
still on, the tough and tender:
long-tailed red beets, slender carrots,
old potatoes with eyes.

The mind shies away from the word
of the teacher, skittish as a colt
that resists the bridle, steps off
as in a dance around the pasture.

But the word is apple, timothy,
a lump of sugar. Trust it.

What holds our breath
is the way the forest grows
without distraction.

*Three*

*In the Medici Chapel*

The tourist carriages stand by outside. Horses
push their noses deep into burlap and oats.
Lorenzo, your streets of patterned stone are
littered with pulltabs and pigeon feathers. We
remind ourselves that dung at least was the same
in your day. Still, your marbles stay magnificent,
cold under our fingers, running smooth bright rivers,
amazing jewels, incredible rainbows. We come here
from the noise of Florence, come indoors to this
rich darkness. Something lulls the heart
stumbling from glory to glory. We marvel.
We shall never see it all. Everything speaks
at the same time, mosaic that flows to one
question we ask you, *sotto voce*, Lorenzo,
how did anyone dream these stones
flowering all together, praising God?

## *Where We Went When We Knew One of Us Would Die*

We went to European cathedrals because she
wanted that, wanted the history of faith
in Gothic arch and medieval stone.
While she could, to walk on floors worn smooth
by the feet of praying generations, to set candles
in alcoves of the saints, be Protestant and anonymous
in the carved pews with polished backs
we couldn't keep from touching.
She wanted the light on Ghiberti's doors,
white marble pietàs.

Twice we went to Fraumünster Kirche in Zurich
where Chagall's windows sang color to God:
Jacob's blue dream with the curving ladder rising
out of its jeweled cave, his sandaled feet set
in a gold ring, Zion the holy city, New Jerusalem
tilted sideways, the Law window pale alongside
the prophets' crimson testimony, and came at last
to Christ, whose window was tall and green.
Seated before these windows, we did not talk.

In Firenze's Church of the Annunciation, we
found a mosaic: the priest blessing mother and son,
an empty fishing boat beside them on the shore,
a purple kerchief around the woman's head,
the priest's arm over the shoulders of the boy
whose face, like the lighthouse in the center,
raised questions of hope and absence.

In the hotel room our last night
before going home to chemo and radiation,
we lay talking of marvels. Sunset broke prisms
over our bodies, stars came out of the deep
Italian dark, and we did not mention weariness,
the hospital.     Or speak of the empty boat.

*Not Lost*

The bells sounding the hours know
where I am, and the sisters have ways,
though we have no words between us.
I listen at the back of their chapel,
pray in my own language to our
mysterious God who is here and not here
and always on the move, not to be caught
in Latin or English or in the holy
statues of the Virgin or any other saint.
The steep cobbled streets acknowledge
my steps and those of the stranger
walking beside me, the one who inhabits
the Umbrian hills and the Northwest rivers
running with perishing salmon, the timeless one
who knows no place and has no name.

*Italian Summer, Thinking of Blueberries*

ripening in August beside the front porch
and greening into blue when I left,
berries *uno e due* on tall stems,
fat clusters heavy at mouth level,
bamboo stakes and ties holding them up

early September mornings I
pick for pleasure and breakfast,
make muffins and cobbler,
fill the freezer for winter,

remember summer on Minnesota lakes,
canoe crossings to islands ripe for plunder,
stripping the ground bushes
of wilder darker fruit we
dropped like edible *pietre preziose*
into buckets and baskets

here there are olives, figs,
and *mirtilli*, blueberries I
want to give to the black-habited sisters
at the convent, invite them
to put down the armloads of linen
they carry across the courtyard
to the laundry room
of Bambin' Gesù

I would like to see their smiles,
their wrinkles and tongues
turning blue

*How Could You Not*

remember the road to Belvedere,
the cloistered sisters behind the stone wall,
the house of friends with an outdoor shower
where your man in love made sacrament
of soap and water, sang cantabile to his Maker,
glad for the body he was glad to be in,
thankful for skin and hair, each pore
and the shining bubbles streaming off,

remember the white towel slapped across his back,
a brisk rubdown between the legs, attention
he gave to balls and cock, each perfectly jointed toe
and finger, his face and neck and ears,
how then, wet towel over his shoulders
he came indoors clean and singing *Ave*
for joy under the wide and open sky,
the cathedral of the world?

*Mysteries in Spoleto*

*When swallows fly in the courtyard, who knows the answer?*
    I didn't hear the question. I didn't hear the question.

*What is time that leaves a record so hard to read?*
    The clock in the tower chimes through an empty face.

*Am I too late for God who turns his back and moves so fast?*
    Stay still. Here, where you are. Someone is looking for you.

*How will I find the street wherever it is I'm going?*
    Carry a light. Walk slow, and go down on your knees.

*If I go down on my knees, what effect will it have?*
    You will bruise them on stone and get up swaying.

*Why did I go back to the Chiesa di San Ansano?*
    To light a candle for John. For him. For so many.

*Who leaves the red bucket in the water trough at the piazza?*
    A woman comes crying at night. You will not see her.

*Why was the pocketbook left on the guardrail and the car lights flashing?*
    When you learn the language you can ask for that story.

*If I knew the language, what would I ask?*
    For all the life I am missing, the red heart of the peach.

*What do the dead take with them? How do they travel?*
    Ask the swallows circling the courtyard. Ask the swallows.

*Foreign Country, Home Country*

You know better. Italian summer will end. You
will return to the country that is your usual
life, underfoot and around you all the time
there as here: in the taverna, the pizzeria,
the slick marble steps of the convent where
many nights you couldn't find the light switch
and pushed alarms the wise sisters ignored.
Underfoot on the local sidewalk as in
the friable stone dust of the Etruscan quarry,
in the town church as in the magnificent Duomo
at Orvieto. You do not have to travel far. Consider
adventure in more familiar country: climbing
the dark streets of your own mind, the risky
intersections with oncoming traffic forcing you
to the wall, the future cutting close. There's native speech
you don't understand, and quirky mistranslations,
nothing wrong with being human. Go home.
There as here, take off your shoes. In your own
backyard, the scraggy spirea bush, burning.

*Four*

*Of Time and Light*

We swim in waters deeper than we know.
Time's fish we are, the current fast and full.
As light recedes, there's nothing much to show.

Foam dies along the beach, the small winds blow.
We can't escape the moon, the tidal pull,
who swim in waters deeper than we know.

Sand sucks at air, the hiss of undertow
a whistle through the socket in the skull.
When light recedes, there's nothing left to show.

The stranded sea stars lose their afterglow.
A hook impales the worm, the silver dulls.
We swim in waters deeper than we know.

Old sailors sing of wreckage far below,
a splintered deck and mainmast, battered hull.
Where light recedes, there's little left to show.

Salt stings the eyes, the creatures merge and flow.
We cannot tell a heron from a gull.
As light recedes we haven't much to show
who swim in waters deeper than we know.

*September Day I Tell to No One*

For months after he died, so ardent I was
on daily walks under redwood and Monterey pine
where for years in many kinds of weather we
stepped on duff and the green needles,
I faced backward on the path, then forward,
said Hammarskjöld's words:
*For all that has been, thanks. For all
that shall be, yes.* Blessing the phrases,
casting their spell into the air,
asking ritual comfort
as if words could be so giving,
heart's repetition be enough.

Today's one more wedding anniversary, and I
live in a different town, in a house I think he'd
like. No less ardent, no less reminded.
Washing windows, I play "Carousel,"
prune bridal wreath that's running wild,
cut the dry rose campion stalks, cross
items off last night's list, my hedge against
the doldrums. I sort papers, photographs,
write a letter to one of the diminished company
who might remember what day this is.

This is one of the days I tell to no one. I don't
know how to begin, where to stop, don't want
sympathy from new or casual friends.
What I want, I take: this slow
inviolate time, these hands-on tasks
that let me follow what rises in the river,
turning where memory takes me,
all day listening to music nobody hears.

*Awake*

when the wind sleeps
and the cricket
goes back to the dark,

when the sea quiets
and the slow waves
have less to say

I tell death
my lust
is enormous

restless
I watch
the new moon

*Word of Honor*

I'll not be faithless in this way, assign
you limits in romance, insist you stay
in songs that break on notes too high,
too sweet to bear, in love's remembered
touch. If death has taken all, death asks
too much, who plays us false in fairytale.
I will not give him that. Not call you
saint or shining knight. You'd laugh

to be in such estate. Instead I claim
your failures, love, and mine, those less
than perfect times, cross-purposed pain
and words ill-said, the chill that kept
the story real. As tears refresh the eye,
the heart, keep vision clear.

*Getting Ready to Move*

Before I go
to recognize each thing
as this, and no other:

my desk with four legs on the floor,
my bed that is only itself, and no ship,
the photograph on the mantel, images

caught in the click of a shutter,
water rippling summer behind us where
we stand with our arms around each other,

the trees fixed in a gold shimmer
already vanishing and crying
*this is the last, this is the last.*

To bring nothing into the house
and to let the things that are here
go. Out of the clutter

that covers space
to give back
clean surfaces.

To save what can be saved
and as I go, to let in the light
of invisible bodies, a memory

touching that shelf, the table
with its grain rising from the wood,
the house sacramental in absence.

*Salt Water*

Small as a snail in the shell of my hand,
in the hollow night on the shore
a child's fingers uncurling, lost
against my palm, my large fingers
with their swollen knuckles,
lines to goodness knows where,
fingers with split and broken nails,
the child I was safe as a snail in the shell
of my hand, closing and opening,
glistening cool in heavy water,
the years sucked down into sand,
pulled under and under, away.

*Return*

Walking through the quiet house, we
take another look at what we thought we saw.

Maybe that's all we're asked to do,
return for another look, one more time
of seeing, saying to ourselves if to no one else,
words we keep learning with our lives.

Going through the motions of going toward
each other, we miss each other. We learn
emptiness from locked rooms, learn that only
because they were filled with noise and presence.

In the nature of things we come back, we have to
come back, unlock the doors and go through
to find what stays open: the full day given again,
mother and father saying words we can hear,
the very words we wanted.

*One Way or Another*

That stranger's smoke, then memory, accessible
and quick: the brand my father used. I'd recognize it
anywhere. Our path divided, and the man was gone.
The wind direction changed.

Since we're houseless after death, and hope to stay
in touch, I want a sign they'll know for certain
that I'm here, but daft on smells I can't decide
which one to travel by.

Lilac late in afternoon? Hot sun on cedar,
eucalyptus, pine? Those pungent human ways
of sweat and salt? Sea air could bring me in.
Lemons. Freesia. Garlic.

Any herb's enough, and never mind how far.
I'd come back safe on fresh-cut summer grass.
Apples. Moldy leaves. The various winds
will have me after all.

*Memory Train*

To reach the past is not easy, you go
so far until, stopped by a face,
a flowering branch, the slant light

through clouds, you stay longer
than you intended. The conductor
calls out station names and you

get off at a place you hadn't planned
to investigate, but you do, then wait
for the next train. They come often

on this busy line, observation cars filled,
people heading back into their lives,
If you go this route, there will be years

to cover, high trestles over canyons,
rivers you crossed once and forgot,
breakdowns, tracks under repair.

On either side of the swaying coach
high-speed trains rush toward the future,
faces blurred behind windows that almost

touch in passing. In either direction, signals
at every crossing. On your ticket, a final
destination: here and now, the present.

*After Eulogies*

tired of praising the dead
as if a body of words could
hold them, provide

a place they'd be content
to live, already they belong
to an order not our own

it's time to send them off
in struck bells, incense,
rising smoke

when we are ready
they come back
white birds

in the branches
of dark pines
beside the water

*Full Stop in the Desert*

Whatever it is we're made for forces you off the freeway,
calls you to attention, requires you to listen
as you've not listened since you were a child
and there were only shimmering transparent veils
between the kingdoms of this world and all the others.

Whatever pulls you toward the red buttes
and the sky is telling you
this much you are permitted to know,
and you can't know what startled you,
brought you to a full stop, nothing asked
but recognition: the exaggerated small sounds,
dust sifting over your shoes, a tumbleweed's
slow roll out of sight.

In the company of wild invisible creatures,
spirits assuming the shape of rocks,
you're not concerned for what comes next
and you can't say how long you stay transfixed
beside the car. If your death is alive in this place
and talking to you, to answer is more than you can.

One or two cars go by and do not stop.
In the shadow of your own car something
compels you to kneel in the dark leaves,
the white flowers of the jimson weed,
the scarlet chuparosa, where you
stammer a few real words, abandon them.
To silence. Whatever it is we are made for.

*Walking My Life*

Striding away from my house when the sun was hot and high
    I came back in rain
with my hair dripping, my feet soaked and my clothes
    stuck to my body.
Light-hearted, head up, and swinging my arms I walked
    on mountain trails
and barefoot in sand beside the sea. For the sake of
    my mother's back
I avoided cracks in the sidewalk and I took giant steps.
    Balancing on steel rails
with the smell of creosote rising around me, I stepped
    up and then down,
from one railroad tie to the next. And through the small
    lights of the dew
that bent the grasses and weighed crystal in the spider's web.
    Carefully, with ice
underfoot, and cross-country on snow-shoes. Under constellations
    calling their names.
Walking and telling stories, I held the hands of my children
    where we followed the sky
across the Golden Gate Bridge and thought we could walk
    into that sky.
On midwest country roads north and east and south and west,
    through towns and great cities.
In unfamiliar villages with foreign words on the signs
    and strange tongues
in the air, I walked in circles. Singing and saying poems,
    talking out loud
to the trees, hoping that without a body you were walking
    with me, I looked

in other faces for the face I loved. On gouged and rutted roads
    of dried clay and over
pebbles and boulders, in my Rockports and Reeboks, my
    Birkenstock sandals
I have counted the miles and gone where the miles
    do not matter.
There is no way to tell how far in this world I have walked
    or to say
what I learn each hour from the blood that moves in its rivers
    and channels
under my skin, from messages delivered to my arms and legs,
    intelligence
received by my eyes and ears, day after day through the delicate
    fine sacs
in my lungs this steady exultant breathing in
    and breathing out.

*Spring Melt*

Crackle of breaking snowcrust
makes lace on the ground, holes
where ice begins to melt

into nests around stone,
leaves of alder,
cottonwood.

Edges of snowpack
thin to crystal mesh,
fine filigree over dirt.

Winter ridges soften
into mud, impressions
from tires, hiking boots.

Each year last year's
cones and needles, broken
limbs and branches

surface on thawing ground.
The river carries light
on its back. March mud

glistens with water. I begin to see
I can no longer walk
in the frozen footprints

of the dead. There is no place
to walk but here, in the slip and slide,
uneasy with questions, holding on.

*Five*

*Summons*

Wasting time as I do
afternoons when I lie down
in a field of oat grass
and chew on a stem while I
watch the summer sky,
the slow way I open my eyes
morning after morning,
you'd not recognize me.

You'd be thinking of that young
busy person with her feelings
breaking open, so sure
of what's right in any argument.
An impossible young woman,
I remember her.

And this other, hiding for years
quiet as a pond at evening.

Now that evening's come
and dark will soon, it's time
to collect my passions and my toys,
summon these lives into one
sweet company
making music while we can.

*Words That Wait to Be Said*

Having come to the place where I
no longer wish to be anyone else,
astonished to find I've traveled
far enough to let the children go

and put the old ladder of perfection
away behind the other antiques
in the barn, what needs me now
is joy, roots in the muddy opposites

I live between. Without apology
the outgrown words of hymns
return me to a lost green morning
of praise and clarity.

Nothing asks to be reconciled.
Arguments settle into dirt
and are covered with grass and flowers.
There are words that wait to be said,

brief testimonies to singular times
when amazement took and shook me
like some rag doll in the mouth
of a great and gentle dog

that can't understand why the floppy thing
refuses to breathe. It is time
to testify, be witness to revelation
while revelation lasts, and before

my sweet life, everything I know
is required, to be traded for dust
or light, my handful of stories
told to air, lost along the way.

*Pittosporum*

In the schoolyard garden the scarecrow's beet-shaped head
    is wrapped in burlap, straw leaks
        from his denim sleeve-ends, a pen oddly
in his pocket, though he is oblivious
    to this growing season or any other
        and will take no notes
on the progress of strawberries,
    sweet corn, the wandering rows of lettuce
        and garlic. *The notes for the poem are*
*the only poem.* Adrienne Rich said, notes I keep
    in trust, as orange-blossom fragrance
        of pittosporum rises
from the dense green hedge beside the path,
    and I remember you liked the smell that followed us
        out of the park. Coming home
to check the *Guide to Shrubs and Trees,* we learned
    that all varieties are evergreen,
        some resistant to drought, and others
adapt to seashore conditions, desert heat,
    learned that "creamy clusters are followed
        by brownish fruits," and "no pittosporum
should be trusted as a foundation plant." Heavier somehow,
    these words I hear now from that other life
        of marriage, the desolation of your dying.

This morning, walking back across the playground,
    walking through white clover and new-cut grass,
        my mind crowded as it sometimes is
with excess of memory out of proportion
    to time, I ask if these notes could become
        a poem, tenuous connections
in convoluted messages
    from pittosporum scent in the air, an absurd
        scarecrow in a school garden.

*Falls River*

Some places intend quiet,
others one word, like *wild*
called out by a musing grandmother
as we stood on the bridge
over the Deschutes, water below us
boiling and spilling so hard and fast
spray flew from the rocks,
stopped our mouths.

If it's true we ought to go
out of our heads at least once a day
this was it for me, as it was a second time
when I looked into the clear pools
holding water and stones,
and then again beside the path
into the pure silence
of the white morning glories.

*Plum*

Though it is early to talk of autumn
the purple asters begin to dry
into decline. Toward the end of summer
something delicious happens on a hot
afternoon when I bend over a blue
china plate to eat a ripe Satsuma plum.
Sticky and sweet, the juice slides off my chin,
the dark skin slips from the red heart
that waits for my teeth as the hard seed
waits for my tongue. A friend said this is
the only way to eat such plums
but love, I did not tell him of a tree
heavy with fruit, year after year
the unforgotten taste of desire.

*Past Lives*

We were in the world before, do you remember that common life,
the details droning like bees in the slow summer?

How could we hide from each other, risk the islands again,
the rocky spines, the core of the volcano? More than

fear or final reproach is the pain of watching us live
our crooked lives now we know what's wrong. You

glance at the letter as if you'd already read it, stand
at the same window, your face that was and is my delight

divided by the crossing bars of the lattice, the pattern
repeating. We were in the world before, and nothing

covers that nakedness, the old armor loose against our flesh,
masks sliding to the floor, our faces the eclipse

of suns, a collapsing star we live on, then as now
deceived by time, memory that escapes us, stays.

*For the Body*

sea-gate to ancient waters,
labyrinth of bones,
grave for the foundered ships
of memory, conduit
to the changing pressure
of tides, uneasy dust
of old stars

when at sundown the sea-gate
closes, when the moon's pull
weakens: be light and empty
as driftwood a long time
on the beach, rise
like rain to the sun,
be vapor in the air

*These Hours Like Making Love*

Living this day is like making love after
long absence, the hours rising and falling
like rain after years of dry weather.
They tumble and slide and are folded
into each other as the new bees of summer
move in and out of the sticky cups
of pink rhododendron, and the heavy
fragrance of lilac breathes a body
of its own. Already I am forgetting
the tag-ends of last night's dread
recurring dream. At the open window
the bare skin of my body
welcomes air that is new, and my eyes
the invitation, sweet daylight come again
bold and delicious with reassurance
I am life's wanton lover still,
besotted by birdsong, giddy with leaves.

*Gratitude*

Filled with the clarity of ancient Chinese poems,
their seasons of plum blossom and peach, wine and exile,
journeys to cities and mountains, years' long sorrow
of parents and lovers, separation by war and politics,
the wisdom of friends in their turning years,
clear evenings and rain on the orchid boats,
I rest in a chair by the window, happy that they
say these things so words are not asked of me
no matter how often I take up my pen hoping
to answer for my life: what is it to you?

## *After Traveling in Kyoto*

Through the barrier gate
crossing the boundary water
toward home that is different and stays
familiar, she gives herself to the ground
like seed into a field. This is her country
and her morning, the calm house,
pages of books her heart leans into,
her unfinished garden, a nameless joy
already going from her
and she can let it go
into patterns
on the raked ocean of stones.

The level of the sea rises.
In this wide and westering light
she stands inside and under,
words come, and for her:
"Be satisfied now
in your body of *samsara*.
Say what is yours to say,
say only that."

And the calm house rocks like a boat.

*Twilight, a Room on Russian Hill*

*for Carolyn*

White orchids in the goldrose light
fading over San Francisco rooftops
clear to the gray hills with other houses,
other rooms. No elegance exact as this
wicker table and Chinese ginger jar
with curly willow, tiny bubbles in a pale
green glass fisherman's float holding light
as if in water, a painted Mexican cat with red
ears, blue and yellow dots spattered like rain.
The orchids are losing light as the sun goes,
they darken to outline, shapes that bend
to an opaque window. They do not now say
*orchid* or *white*, they have folded their tongues,
relinquished definition, the orange flush
at the heart, a white perfection of petals.

*Questions Before Dark*

Day ends, and before sleep
when the sky dies down, consider
your altered state: has this day
changed you? Are the corners
sharper or rounded off? Did you
live with death? Make decisions
that quieted? Find one clear word
that fit? At the sun's midpoint
did you notice a pitch of absence,
bewilderment that invites
the possible? What did you learn
from things you dropped and picked up
and dropped again? Did you set a straw
parallel to the river, let the flow
carry you downstream?

*Praise What Comes*

surprising as unplanned kisses, all you haven't deserved
of days and solitude, your body's immoderate good health
that lets you work in many kinds of weather. Praise

talk with just about anyone. And quiet intervals, books
that are your food and your hunger, nightfall and walks
before sleep. Praising these for practice, perhaps

you will come at last to praise grief and the wrongs
you never intended. At the end there may be no answers
and only a few very simple questions: did I love,

finish my task in the world? Learn at least one
of the many names of God? At the intersections,
the boundaries where one life began and another

ended, the jumping-off places between fear and
possibility, at the ragged edges of pain,
did I catch the smallest glimpse of the holy?